Enid Blyton's

MAGICAL TALES

The Wonderful Teddy Bear

and other stories

This is a Parragon Book

© Parragon 1997

13-17 Avonbridge Trading Estate,
Atlantic Road, Avonmouth, Bristol
Produced by The Templar Company plc,
Pippbrook Mill, London Road, Dorking,
Surrey RH4 1JE

Text copyright © Enid Blyton Ltd 1926-29

These stories were first published in Sunny Stories,
Teacher's Treasury, Two Years in the Infant School,
Read to Us, New Friends and Old and
The Daily Mail Annual.

Enid Blyton's signature mark is a registered
trademark of Enid Blyton Limited.

Edited by Caroline Repchuk and Dugald Steer

Designed by Mark Kingsley-Monks

Printed and bound in Italy

ISBN 0 7525 1703 1 (Hardback)
ISBN 0 7525 2318 X (Paperback)

Enid Blyton's

The Wonderful Teddy Bear

and other stories

Contents

The Wonderful Teddy Bear

ONCE there was a fat little teddy bear who lived in the toy cupboard. He thought rather a lot of himself, especially as he could do several things that he thought were rather clever.

"I can tie a bow," he said. "Look, I can tie your ribbon in your hair, Rosebud. Stand still, and I'll tie it."

He tied quite a nice bow, and talked about it for a whole day.

"I can thread beads, too," he said, when another doll's bead necklace broke. "Angela, I'll thread your necklace again and you can wear it."

So he picked up the beads and

threaded them for Angela. She was pleased, but Teddy spoilt it by boasting about the necklace all day long.

"I mended it," he kept saying. "I picked up all the beads. I threaded them on some cotton. I am really very, very clever."

"You would be cleverer if you didn't boast," said the sailor doll. "If you ever *mention* beads again I shall chase you round and round the table till you fall over. Go over there into the corner and be quiet."

"But why *should* I be quiet?" asked Teddy. "I'm clever, and I like to talk. It would do you a lot

of good if you listened to me,
Sailor Doll."

"I've gone deaf," said the sailor
doll, putting his hands over his
ears. "I can't hear you!"

And wasn't it annoying for
Teddy when all the other toys
giggled and covered their ears
up, too!

So, however much Teddy told
them about all the clever things
he could do, nobody was able to
hear him.

Then one day he found a card
lying on the floor of the
playroom. The children had been
playing a game of cards earlier
that day and had dropped one of

them. Teddy picked it up and looked at the picture on the other side.

Oh, what a fine picture he saw! It was a picture of a fat little teddy bear, dressed in a top hat, a smart bow, and carrying a walking stick! Underneath it were four words:

THE WONDERFUL
TEDDY BEAR

"There!" said Teddy in delight. "Here's my picture! My very own picture – and look what it says underneath – 'The Wonderful Teddy Bear.' That's me! Oh, I *must* hurry and show it to the other toys!"

So he hurried to show it to Rosebud and Angela and the sailor doll and the clown and the wobbly man and all the rest.

"Look! This is me! *Now* will you admit how clever and wonderful I am? Look at my top hat – and my fine walking cane – and my beautiful bow! I'm 'The Wonderful Teddy Bear'!"

They all looked.

"But you haven't *got* a top hat and a walking stick," said the sailor doll. "And you'd look silly if you had."

"I would not," said Teddy. "And what is more, I think I would look fine with them. I think

I *ought* to have them. I think you ought to buy them for me."

"Well, you can go on thinking," said the sailor doll. "Anyway, that's only a picture."

"But it's a picture of *me*!" said Teddy. "'The Wonderful Teddy Bear.' It says so underneath. It's my very own picture, the artist must have meant it for me. He must know me."

"Rubbish," said the sailor doll. "I don't believe it."

But Teddy went on and on about his picture. He didn't know it was a playing card. He pinned it up inside the toy cupboard so that he could look at it all day long and the other toys got very tired of seeing it stuck there.

And then one day the sailor doll found the whole pack of cards in a box! There they were – cards showing dolls and bears and clowns and all the rest. The sailor doll looked at them very carefully indeed.

He found three more cards showing teddy bears. One showed a teddy bear sitting in a corner, looking very sad. Underneath the picture four words were written:

THE NAUGHTY
TEDDY BEAR

Then the sailor doll looked at

the next card. It showed a teddy
bear stealing some sweets from
the the toy sweet shop.
Underneath it four words were
written again:

THE WICKED
TEDDY BEAR

And on the last card was a
picture of a teddy bear running
away from a little clockwork
mouse. Underneath it were four
words again:

THE SILLY TEDDY BEAR

Dear me, how the sailor doll
giggled. He looked round and
saw that the fat little teddy bear
was away at the other end of the
room, telling the clockwork

mouse how brave he was.

The sailor doll took down the picture of THE WONDERFUL TEDDY BEAR and pinned up the other three instead. Then he sat and waited.

Soon the other toys caught sight of the three cards and they went to have a look at them. How astonished they were!

"Oooh, look – isn't Teddy a coward? – he's being chased by the clockwork mouse – he's very, very silly. And do look – how very shocking, he's stealing sweets out of the toy sweet shop. Ha – no wonder he's called Wicked. And in this one he has been put into the corner because he's been bad. That's where *we* should put him when he makes a nuisance of himself."

Teddy came up. He had got himself a smart bow and a little stick, but he hadn't been able to find a top hat. He swung his stick as he came up. "What are you looking at? My wonderful picture?" he asked, proudly.

"Yes, we're looking at some pictures of you," said the sailor doll, with a giggle. "They're much more like you than the other one you pinned up."

"Oh! Oh! Look at me, chasing him!" cried the clockwork

mouse, and he laughed so much that his key fell out.

"And my goodness me – he's stealing sweets," said Rosebud, shocked. "If he does that kind of thing I'll certainly never speak to him again!"

"Let's put him in the corner, like he is in *this* picture!" said the sailor doll, trying to be stern and not giggle.

Teddy stared at the three pictures in the greatest astonishment and alarm! Goodness! How had they got there? Where was the beautiful picture of him in the top hat and the lovely bow? These were quite dreadful!

"They're not me!" he cried. "They're not!"

"But it says they are!" said the clockwork mouse. "And it's the same teddy bear in these pictures as it is in the one you first showed us. It *is* you!"

"Who would have thought Teddy was so bad?" asked the wobbly man, really shocked. "I really *do* think we ought to put him in the corner."

Teddy crept away on tiptoe to a corner of the playroom. He took off his smart bow, and threw away his walking stick. Then he went back to the toys.

"Please," he said, "if I say that the first picture wasn't me after all, will you say that these aren't me either?"

"You mean that if we don't believe these pictures are of you, you won't believe the one of the wonderful bear is you either?" asked the sailor doll.

"Yes," said Teddy, humbly. "I'm not bad or wicked or silly – but I'm not really wonderful, either. So please *do* take those pictures away!"

The sailor doll took them down and put them back in the box where he had found them. But he was giggling so much as he put them away that the toy clown begged him to tell him what the joke was.

"Well, turn round and look at the clockwork mouse," said the sailor doll, laughing. "He's chasing Teddy round and round the table! *He* thinks that one of the pictures is real, anyhow!"

Poor little teddy bear! He never once boasted again, which was a very good thing. But the clockwork mouse chased him so often that in the end the sailor doll had to take his key out.

He *does* have to keep the toys in order, doesn't he!

One Day
After Tea

PETER had taken his clockwork motor car out into the garden. He wound it up and set it running over the grass. It bumped here and there, and then ran straight on to the flower bed and turned over.

Peter spoke to the little man at the wheel. "You're the driver, aren't you? Surely you can at least drive the car properly, and steer it away from the beds?"

The little man said nothing. He wasn't alive, so he couldn't. He was only a toy. Peter set the car upright again, under the garden seat. "That's a parking place," he told the little man. "Park there till I come back."

He went off for his tea. The car stayed quietly parked under the seat. A small voice suddenly spoke in the driver's ear.

"I *say*! Does that motor car really *go*?"

The driver looked straight in front of him and didn't answer. There was a little tinkling laugh and a tiny brownie came around to the front of the car and looked into his face.

"Oh! You want a spell rubbed on you to make you alive, don't you? Well, here goes!"

Something was rubbed over the toy driver and he suddenly

felt quite different. He blinked his eyes. He stretched his legs. He turned to look at the brownie.

"Hello," said the brownie. "I asked you a question just now. Does this car really go?"

"Yes, of course," said the driver. "But you have to wind it up first."

"You wind it up then," said the brownie. So the toy driver got out and began turning the key. And while he was busy winding, the brownie slipped into the driver's seat and sat there waiting!

When the car was wound up, the toy driver let go the key – and the car shot off with the brownie driving it! Down the garden it went, going towards the hedge with the astonished toy driver after it, running for the first time in his life!

"Hey! Come back! That's not your car! Come back!"

The brownie laughed loudly, shot through the hedge and drove the car straight down a rabbit hole. The toy driver was very upset. Whatever would Peter say?

"Somehow I must get it back before Peter misses it," thought the little driver. "Even if it means going down that hole. I'm really very scared."

Still, he couldn't allow anyone

to rush off with his car like that, so through the hedge he went, and down the hole.

He met a large rabbit and couldn't imagine what it was. He squeezed himself against the wall of the hole so that the rabbit could pass.

"I suppose you haven't seen a little car down here, have you?" he asked, politely.

"Yes, I have," said the rabbit, rather crossly. "It came tearing down at top speed, hooting loudly, and nearly ran me over. It's that tiresome little brownie again. He's always doing rude things like that."

"Does he live down here?" asked the driver.

"Yes – the third door on the left," said the rabbit. "You'll probably find the car outside, as he certainly can't take it in."

The toy driver went on down the hole. He passed one door labelled 'Mrs Floppy'. Another door was called 'Mr Brownie', but the toy driver didn't bother to read the name because outside, all by itself, stood his little car.

He could hear an excited voice on the other side of the door. "I've got a most beautiful car! Do come for a ride in it!"

The toy driver frowned. So the

brownie thought it was *his* car now, did he? Well, he would soon know better.

He slipped into the driving seat, and then got out again. Bother! The car was run down. He would have to wind it up again. So he wound it up and then jumped quickly into the front seat. R-r-r-r-r-r! Off went the car, speeding down the rabbit hole, because the driver hadn't had time to turn it round and go the other way.

This was dreadful. Wherever was he going? It was dark and the tunnels wound in and out of each other. He turned into a tunnel that led upwards, and the car shot away, up and up, and then out into the open air! It stopped suddenly.

The driver got out and wound it up again. He saw a hedge nearby, and drove to the little gap there. In he went, and was *very* relieved to find he had driven back into Peter's garden! He really felt very glad indeed.

Now he would get back to the seat before Peter came – but wasn't that Peter sitting there, his legs swinging to and fro? Yes, it was. Could the little driver get underneath the seat without being seen?

He drove up carefully, ran gently into one of the seat's legs and stopped. Peter heard him, of course, and looked down.

"Well!" he cried in surprise. "Wherever did you come from? I've been looking for you everywhere! Do you mean to say you wound up the car by yourself, went for a ride, and came back here? How marvellous!"

He wound the car up, and looked at the little toy driver. "You look different somehow," he said. "I wonder why? Now – if you can go off by yourself and come back as you did, let me see you drive *properly*!"

Well, of course, the little driver *could* drive properly now, and he took the car down the path and back and ended up at Peter's feet. "Splendid!" said Peter, pleased. "You've really learnt to drive."

So he had of, course, and now he drives the toys at top speed round the playroom every night, and never bumps into anything.

But when he's out in the garden with the car, he keeps a sharp look-out for the brownie. He's going to hoot loudly and tell him just what he thinks of him, if he ever sees him, just to show him what happens to people who steal toy cars!

Away goes
his Head!

"RUBBALONG!" called Ma. "Where are you? I want you to get on with that bit of garden today – the piece that's all stony."

"Right, Ma," said little Rubbalong. "I'll go and have a look at it." So off he went – but, oh dear, how very stony it was! Nothing would ever grow there with so many stones, that was certain. Rubbalong sighed when he thought how hard he would have to work.

"It will take me hours to collect those stones and throw them over the wall," groaned Rubbalong. "I really must think of some way to get rid of them."

Well, he sat down and thought very hard indeed. Then he got up and went indoors. He set to work with an old broom-handle and a big round saucepan without a handle and with a hole in the bottom, that Ma Rubbalong never used.

He stuck the saucepan on the end of the broom-handle. The handle was just a bit bigger than the hole in the saucepan, so when it was forced through, it stuck there nicely.

Then little Rubbalong painted a marvellous face on the old saucepan – a face whose big eyes shone, and whose big mouth grinned.

Then he pulled handfuls of hair from an old rug and made a shock of hair for the saucepan face. Really, it looked most remarkable when he had finished with it.

"What *do* you think you're doing, little Rubbalong?" said his mother. "What a dreadful face! Are you making a scarecrow or something?"

"You wait and see, Ma," said little Rubbalong. He took the broom-handle and saucepan head outside into the garden. Then he climbed carefully over the wall with it, and stuck it firmly into the ground just beyond the wall.

The odd, grinning face with its shock of hair looked over the wall in a most peculiar way.

Rubbalong chuckled. He took up a stone and threw it at the face. He missed. He picked up another and missed again. Soon Mister Tuck-In came along and Clang, the blacksmith.

"You're a bad shot," said Mr Tuck-In. "Let *me* have a go." In an instant he was standing beside little Rubbalong in the garden, picking up stones and throwing them at the saucepan face as fast as he could.

But he missed every time. Clang, the blacksmith was a better shot. He hit the face with a big stone and it made a loud clanging noise that startled the blacksmith very much.

"Good shot!" cried Rubbalong. "You hit him – but can you throw so hard that you knock his head right off? Ah – you want good aim and strength for that, Mr Clang!"

Button the pixie came along. So did Dame Scary and Mrs Chatter. Mrs Well-I-Never came and many others. As soon as they saw Mr Tuck-In and Mr

Clang throwing stones at the silly saucepan head, they all wanted to have a go too.

"Clang!" That was a lucky shot of Mrs Scary's. "Clang!" That was one from Button. "CLANG!" That was the blacksmith again, and his stone struck the head so hard that it wobbled on its broom-handle.

"Nearly got it off that time!" shouted Mr Clang with excitement, and he picked up a great pocketful of stones to throw.

Soon there was quite a crowd of people throwing at the saucepan head. Rubbalong chuckled to see how clean the

piece of garden was getting –
nearly all the stones were gone
now. What a fine way of ridding
a garden of its stones!

"CLANG!" The blacksmith
had hurled such a big stone, and
aimed so well that the saucepan
head flew right off its handle and
disappeared.

"DONE IT!" roared Clang in
delight. Rubbalong clapped him
on the back. "Well done!" he
said. "You've won. Come along
in and have a slice of Ma's new
chocolate cake!"

When Clang had gone, and all
the others had disappeared,
Rubbalong showed his mother

the piece of garden. "There you are, Ma," he said. "Hardly a stone left. Our kind friends did all the work for me."

"You played a trick on them, little Rubbalong," said Ma. "You made them do your work for you. You had better be careful that they don't scold you for it when they see you digging over that bit of garden and doing your planting."

Well, Rubbalong dug the piece of garden over. He planted lettuce seeds and radish seeds. He sowed turnip seeds and carrots. He watered it and weeded it, and my goodness me, how that little bit of garden grew and flourished.

Great fat lettuces, sturdy, round radishes, and turnips all swelled up, waving their green, tufty heads. Little Rubbalong was delighted.

And then Mr Clang spoke angrily to him. "Ha! *We* did the work in that garden for you! *We* prepared it by getting rid of all those stones. And now you have a whole garden full of fine vegetables. That was a trick, Rubbalong."

"Yes, it was," said little Rubbalong. "And I'm very grateful to you all. Everybody who threw a stone at the old saucepan head is going to get a present from my garden. Thank you for your help, Mr Clang. Here is a fat lettuce for you, a bunch of radishes, and a fine turnip for your soup!"

Well, little Rubbalong took all his friends the same present, and they were delighted. "Play all the tricks you like if this is the kind of reward we get!" said Button, the pixie. "Hurrah!"

Have *you* a bit of stony garden? Ask Rubbalong to lend you that old saucepan head then. You'll know just what to do with it now!

Peter Penny

PETER Penny, the gnome, was most tremendously pleased with himself. He had saved up all his money until he had enough to buy a white rabbit to ride on.

So he went to market and bought one. It was a lovely one, as soft as silk and white as snow. He climbed up onto its back to ride home.

"Off you go!" he cried. And off the rabbit went, lolloping along through the wood. Peter Penny thought it was lovely.

After a little while he met Skippetty Wee, who carried a darling little yellow bird under his arm. Peter Penny got off his rabbit and looked at it.

"What sort of bird is that?" he asked, curiously.

"It's a Dobbady Bird," said Skippetty. "She lays an egg for your breakfast and an egg for your tea every day. And fancy, Peter, if you have a friend to tea, she will lay you an extra egg!"

Peter thought it was the most incredible bird he had ever heard of. He wished he had one too.

"Look at my new rabbit," he said to Skippetty.

Skippetty looked at it.

"All very fine," he said, "but it can't lay eggs!"

"No," said Peter Penny, looking rather upset; "it can't."

"Look here," said Skippetty. "I know you love eggs. As you're a great friend of mine, I'll change my bird for your rabbit, if you like. Then you'll have eggs to eat every day!"

Peter Penny thought of new-laid eggs every day, and his mouth watered.

"All right," he said, handing Skippetty the reins of his rabbit; "I'll change over. Give me the Dobbady Bird."

So Skippetty gave him the little Dobbady Bird, mounted Peter's lovely white rabbit, waved his hand, and rode away.

Peter Penny went on through the wood, carrying the bird, and thinking of new-laid eggs. Presently he met Jinkie the Pixie, who stopped and wished him good afternoon.

"Good afternoon," said Peter. "Look at my Dobbady Bird. She lays an egg for breakfast, an egg for tea, and an extra one if you have a friend visiting! Fancy that!"

"Goodness!" said Jinkie. "Fancy eating eggs every single day! How tired you'll get of them, Peter Penny!"

"Oh dear, I hope not," said Peter Penny anxiously.

"Well, you will," said Jinkie. "Look here, and see what *I've* got! This is better than eggs twice every day!"

He put his hand in his pocket, and pulled out a little mouse that blinked up at Peter Penny with bright black eyes.

"Oh, it's a dear little mouse!" said Peter Penny. "But whatever good is a mouse, Jinkie?"

"I'll tell you," said Jinkie. "He eats up all the crumbs that drop down on the floor, Peter, so you don't have to keep on sweeping them up! Isn't that good! It saves such a lot of work, you know."

Now, Peter Penny was a very

untidy eater. He dropped crumbs
on to the floor at every meal, and
was always having to sweep them
up afterwards. He thought the
little mouse was a splendid idea.

Jinkie guessed what Peter was
thinking.

"Listen, Peter Penny," he said.
"You're a very great friend of
mine, so I'll tell you what I'll do.
I will give you my mouse in
exchange for your Dobbady
Bird. You will never have to
sweep up crumbs again!"

"All right," said Peter Penny,
handing Jinkie the little bird;
"I'll swap with you. Give me the
little mouse."

So Jinkie gave him the mouse, took the Dobbady Bird, waved his hand, and went on his way.

Peter Penny walked on through the wood with the little mouse in his pocket, thinking how nice it would be not to have to sweep up crumbs any more.

Soon he met Oll the Goblin, who was whistling just like a blackbird on a little silver flute.

"Good afternoon," said Peter Penny. "Look at my little mouse. He will eat up all the crumbs I drop from my table, so that I don't need to sweep them up. Fancy that!"

"My, my!" said Oll. "Fancy

keeping a tame mouse when you live next door to Witch Wimple and her cat. Why, the cat will sniff it out and eat it in ten minutes!"

"Oh dear! I hadn't thought of that," said Peter Penny, very worried. "Whatever shall I do?"

Oll blew a merry tune on his flute. It sounded just like a lark.

"Dear me!" said Peter Penny, "that's a fine flute! At first when I met you, it sounded just like a blackbird! Now it sounds exactly like a lark!"

"And now it sounds like a canary!" said Oll, blowing it –and it did. Then he made it sound like a yellow-hammer, and

then a nightingale, till Peter
could hardly believe his ears.

"I wish I'd got a flute instead of
a mouse!" he sighed.

Oll laughed.

"Well, as you're a great friend
of mine," he said, "I'll tell you
what I'll do. I'll give you my flute
in exchange for your mouse."

"All right," said Peter Penny,
very pleased. He handed over
the mouse. Oll gave him the
flute, put the mouse in his
pocket, waved his hand, and ran
off into the woods.

Peter Penny walked on
through the wood with the flute
hung round his neck, thinking

how fine it would be to whistle like a bird.

Soon he met Trippit the Elf. She stopped and wished him good afternoon.

"Good afternoon," said Peter Penny. "Look at my wonderful flute. It whistles like any bird you care to mention when I blow on it. What do you think of *that*?"

"Not much!" said Trippit. "What's the use of whistling like a bird? You just use up all your breath, and it makes you feel quite hungry."

"Oh dear!" said Peter Penny. "Does it really? I already get so hungry I can hardly make my money last. Dear, dear, dear!"

"Just look at what *I've* got!" said Trippit, taking out a little packet. She opened it, and there lay a little steel needle.

"Well, it's only a needle!" said Peter Penny.

"Ah, but listen!" said Trippit. "It's a wonderful needle. It will mend any hole in your stockings or your clothes all by itself. What do you think of *that*?"

"Marvellous!" said Peter Penny, thinking of all his torn clothes at home that he never had time to mend. "Does it really, now! How I wish I had a useful thing like that!"

"Well," said Trippit the Elf, "I'll tell you what I'll do, Peter Penny. You're a great friend of mine, so if you like, I'll give you my needle in exchange for your whistling flute!"

"Oh, thank you," cried Peter Penny. He handed over his flute and took the needle. Trippit waved and ran off merrily, playing the flute so that it sounded like a thrush singing after the rain.

Peter Penny went on through the wood, thinking of what a fine time he would have when he set his needle to work, mending all his clothes. He was so busy thinking about it that he didn't look where he was going, and very soon he was lost.

"Oh dear!" cried Peter Penny miserably, "I'm lost – and the night is coming on – and I'm cold and hungry. Oh dear, dear!"

He wandered on through the woods for a long time, feeling very tired and cross, but not a house could he see, and not a person did he meet.

At last he sat down on a stone, and cried and cried and cried.

An old witch, riding by on a broomstick, heard him crying, and came down to see what was the matter.

"I'm lost!" said Peter Penny. "I

live on Blowaway Hill, and I
don't know how to get there. Will
you take me home on your
broomstick?"

"Oho!" said the witch. "This
needs thinking about. What will
you give me if I do?"

"Can't you be nice and do it for
nothing, out of kindness?" asked
Peter Penny.

"I'm not a nice person," said
the witch, "and only nice people
do things for nothing. Give me a
silver coin, and then I will take
you home."

"I haven't any money left,"
said Peter Penny. "I spent it all at
the market."

"What did you buy?" asked the witch.

"A rabbit to ride home on," answered Peter.

"Well, why *didn't* you ride home on it?" asked the witch.

"Because I changed it for a Dobbady Bird, that could lay eggs twice a day," Peter told her.

"Oho! And where's the wonderful bird?" asked the witch, looking all round.

"I changed it for a little mouse that would eat up all the crumbs I dropped," said Peter, sadly.

"Where's the mouse, then?" asked the witch.

"I haven't got it," answered

Peter Penny mournfully. "I changed it for a magic flute."

"Oho! A magic flute!" said the witch. "Let me hear you play a tune, and then I'll take you home."

"I haven't got that either," said Peter, beginning to feel foolish. "I changed it for a needle that could mend holes by itself! Here it is."

He showed it to the witch. Her eyes glistened.

"I'll take you home if you give me that," she told him.

"No!" said Peter. "I want it."

"All right," said the witch, "I'm going." And she jumped on to her broomstick.

"Stop! Stop!" cried Peter in a panic. "Don't leave me. I'll give you my magic needle, really I will, if you'll just take me home!"

The witch took his needle, and told him to jump on to the broomstick. Then away they went right up into the air as fast as the wind.

Peter Penny held on to the broomstick as tightly as ever he could. He wasn't a bit used to riding on sticks, and it felt terribly uncomfortable"

"What a horrid way of getting home!" he thought. "Why ever didn't I keep my white rabbit, instead of changing it? I could have ridden home very comfortably on that."

On and on they went, with the wind whistling in Peter Penny's ears and taking his breath away.

Then phuff! Off flew his favourite cap into the night and was lost for ever.

"Oh my goodness!" thought Peter dolefully. "There goes my nice new cap that I bought only last week! But I daren't ask the witch to stop to look for it. She might leave me behind on the ground."

So he said nothing about his cap, and on and on they went again into the night.

Just as Peter was getting so
cold that he thought he really
couldn't hold on to the
broomstick any longer with his
cold hands, he saw Blowaway
Hill just below them. The
broomstick glided slowly down,
and bump, there was Peter at
home again.

Before he could say a word, the
witch had flown off again, taking
his magic needle safely with her.

Peter Penny was very, very sad.
He went into his little house and
made himself a nice cup of hot
cocoa. Then he undressed and
got into bed.

And all the night he dreamed

of the soft white rabbit he might have ridden on, the Dobbady Bird who would have lain him mountains of eggs, the little mouse who would have eaten his crumbs, the flute that would have whistled like a bird, and the needle that would have mended his clothes.

Then he woke with a jump, and cried big tears into his pillow. "I've been silly," he wept; "but I won't be silly any more."

And you will be glad to hear that he hasn't been silly since then, not even once. So his unhappy adventure brought him *some* good after all.

When Mother Lost Her Purse

THERE was a circus in the village. Betty and Jack had seen the caravans coming along, and had heard the lions roaring. They had even seen a clown turning head-over-heels in the road. "And once he went splash in a puddle!" laughed Betty, telling her mother all she had seen. "Wouldn't it be lovely if we could go and see him at the circus. I would so love to."

"Oh, Mother, can we?" asked Jack. "Do, do take us. We've been ever so good this week, haven't we?"

"Yes, you have," answered Mother, smiling. "Well, I'll take

you both this evening!"

"Oh! Oh! Oh! How lovely!" cried Jack and Betty, dancing round in delight.

"We'll see the lions!" shouted Jack merrily.

"And the clown!" cried Betty.

Mother laughed. "Yes, it *will* be great fun!" she said. "Run off to school now, dears, or you'll be late."

Jack and Betty went off to school, and told everyone that they were going to the circus that evening. They could hardly sit still, they were so excited. They kept thinking of lions and horses, elephants and clowns, until they seemed to see them dancing all over their books.

They rushed home to tea as fast as their legs could carry them, and burst into the house like runaway ponies.

"Mother! Mother!" They cried. "How long is it till we go to the circus?"

Mother was in the kitchen, taking some hot currant cakes out of the oven. She turned to greet them and tried to smile, but her eyes looked sorrowful.

"My dears," she said, "I've got a terrible disappointment for you. We can't go to the circus after all."

"Oh, Mother! Why ever not?" asked Jack in dismay.

"I've lost my purse," said Mother sadly. "I went out shopping this afternoon, and when I got home I couldn't find my purse. I must have dropped it in the road, but when I went to look for it, I couldn't find it anywhere."

"Was there a lot of money in it?" asked Jack.

"Yes," said Mother. "And now that I've lost it, I can't afford to take you to the circus, you see. I'm dreadfully sorry, dears."

"Poor old Mother," said Jack, putting his arm round her.

"Never mind. *We* don't mind."

Betty began to cry.

"*I* mind," she sobbed. "Haven't you got some other money somewhere to take us with, Mother?" asked Betty. "You did promise, you know."

"Be quiet, Betty," said Jack. "We aren't babies, to cry over a little disappointment."

"It *isn't* a little disappointment, it's a big one," answered Betty, truthfully. But she dried her eyes. If Jack was going to be brave, she was too.

"I've made you some lovely hot currant cakes for tea," said Mother, kissing Betty. "Let's all try hard and forget our disappointment and be really brave about it. We're none of us babies, are we!"

"No, we're not!" said Jack. "Cheer up, Betty. Let's go out and play a game in the garden before tea."

"You've got just half an hour," said Mother. "I wonder if you'd mind sweeping up some of those fallen leaves in the front garden for me? I noticed how terribly untidy they were when I came in earlier."

"Come on, Betty, we'll go and tidy them all up!" cried Jack, trying to be cheerful. He took hold of Betty's arm and pulled her out of doors.

"I don't feel like doing anything like that," said Betty miserably.

"Nor do I," said Jack. "But think how poor Mother must feel. She is just as disappointed as we are, so let's do something to cheer *her* up. I know she'd be pleased to see the front garden nice and tidy."

"All right," said Betty, trying to smile. "I'll go and get the wheelbarrow, Jack. You fetch the brooms."

Soon both children were as busy as busy could be. Jack

swept the leaves into big heaps
and Betty lifted them into the
wheelbarrow. When it was full,
they wheeled it over to the
rubbish-heap and emptied the
load out there.

It was very hard work, but
neither of the children was lazy.
They had emptied two barrows,
and were filling the third when
something fell with a loud thud
against the side of the barrow,
just as Betty threw in a pile of
crackly leaves.

"You've found a chestnut!" said
Jack. "Look and see. It might be
a good one. The wind has blown
lots down among the leaves."

Betty looked. She could not see anything. She put her hand in among the dry, crackly leaves and felt about.

"I can't feel anything," she was beginning to say, when suddenly her hand closed on something that felt quite hard.

She pulled it out and looked at it. It wasn't a chestnut. Oh no! It was something much lovelier than that.

"Jack! Jack!" squeaked Betty, so suddenly that Jack dropped his broom in fright. "Look! It's Mother's purse! And it's still full of money!"

"Hurrah! Hurrah!" shouted

Jack. "Mother must have dropped it in the garden and the piles of leaves hid it. Hurrah!"

"Come on and tell Mother!" cried Betty, too excited to stand still. She and Jack ran into the house, shouting at the tops of their voices.

"Goodness gracious!" said Mother in alarm. "Whatever is the matter?"

"Your purse, your purse!" shouted the children. "We found it in the leaves!'

"Oh, how lovely!" said Mother, taking her purse and opening it. "And all the money is safe. We can go to the circus, after all!"

"It's too good to be true!" said Jack, bursting with delight.

"And just think, my dears," said Mother suddenly, "if you hadn't been brave and unselfish over your disappointment, you wouldn't have tidied the garden for me - and then you wouldn't have found my purse!"

"But we *have* found it; we *have* found it!" cried Betty. "Let's hurry up and have tea and go!"

And very soon off they went to the circus. They had the most wonderful time watching the lovely dancing horses and the roaring lions. The clowns made them laugh so hard that they thought their sides would burst. They clapped and cheered and wished that the circus could last forever. But at last it came to an end and it was time for them to go home to bed.

"Thank you, Mother," said Jack. "We had a perfectly wonderful time."

"Thank you, dears. If you had not found my purse we would all have missed the fun," answered Mother.

They chattered brightly all the way home and they all agreed it was the very nicest circus in the world. And I really think they deserved it, don't you?

Mother Winkyns Washing

THERE was once an old lady called Mother Winkyn, who lived all alone with her black cat in a little cottage. She was a grumpy old thing, and never had a smile or a kind word for any boy or girl. As for giving any of them a penny, she never so much as thought of it.

"Boys and girls are just a nuisance," she would grumble to herself. "Noisy, shouting creatures! I don't like them at all. They are rude and selfish!"

Well, of course, you couldn't expect any boy or girl to like Mother Winkyn either. They kept themselves away from her.

None of them offered to go on errands for her, and not one of them said "Good morning," or smiled at her, for they were really quite afraid of her.

Now one morning Mother Winkyn did her washing and pegged it out on the line in her garden. It was a very windy morning, so she knew it would dry nice and quickly.

"I'll just put on my bonnet and go to do my shopping whilst my washing dries," said Mother Winkyn. So off she went with her basket, and left her line of washing dancing madly in the March wind.

No sooner had she turned the corner than the wind swooped down on the washing once again and began to tug at Mother Winkyn's best yellow petticoat, the one she always wore under her best Sunday frock. This petticoat was pegged up in the middle of the line of washing, and Mother Winkyn was very proud of it.

The wind tugged and tugged at it, and at last the petticoat flew from the pegs that held it and went sailing down the street. The boys and girls playing in the street saw it, and called out in delight.

"There goes Mother Winkyn's washing! Oh, look! There goes Mother Winkyn's washing!"

But one little boy looked rather worried.

"Oh dear!" he said. "Shouldn't we go after it? It will get lost. My mother was very upset once when a pair of my pyjamas blew away and was lost."

"Fiddlesticks! Let Mother Winkyn's washing *get* lost!" cried the other children. "Don't worry about her. She really is a horrid old thing!"

"All the same, I don't like to see the things blown away like that," said the little boy, as he watched the yellow petticoat dance away down the street. "I think I'll go after it and bring it back for her."

So off went the kind-hearted boy, and tried to catch the petticoat up. But as soon as he got near it the wind picked it up and blew it just a little farther on. It flew over the hedge and into a field. It landed on top of a cow, who was quietly eating lunch, and frightened it so much that it galloped round the field with the yellow petticoat hanging on its horns.

Then the petticoat dropped off, and the little boy ran across the field to pick it up. Puff! The wind swept down again and off went the petticoat over the stream nearby, all the way to the field on the other side.

"Bother it!" said the little boy, quite determined now to get hold of that petticoat somehow. He found a narrow place and jumped across the stream. Then he ran towards the yellow petticoat which was still lying there in a flat heap on the grass. Puff! The wind blew down again and the petticoat danced off in the breeze once more!

This time it flew towards the lane that led to the shops. On and on it went and the little boy ran after it as fast as he could. It sailed over a fence and into the lane. Then it danced round the corner towards where the baker's shop was.

The little boy raced after it. He rushed round the corner and bumped straight into someone, knocking her over and sending her basket flying!

"Oh, bother you, you clumsy, careless creature!" cried a cross voice. "Look what you've gone and done!"

The little boy looked. He was sorry that he had knocked somebody down – and dear me,

who do you think it was?
It was Mother Winkyn coming
back from her shopping with her
basket of onions, potatoes,
oranges and apples! They were
spilt all over the road and were
rolling in all directions.

"Now you just pick them all up
for me," scolded Mother
Winkyn. "And then you come
along with me and I'll complain
to your mother how you rush
about and knock people over,
you horrid rough child!"

The little boy was frightened.
He picked up all the oranges,
apples, onions and potatoes and
put them into the basket. Then

he looked round for the petticoat. Ah, there it was, huddling in the doorway of the baker's shop. He rushed to it and caught it before the wind could send it flying into the air again. He bundled it under his arm and went back to Mother Winkyn, meaning to give it to her. But she had thought he was going to run off with it and she was very cross.

"Did you hear what I said?" she scolded. "I'm going to make you come back with me and I'll tell your mother what a badly-behaved child you are. Throw that yellow rag down. What do you want to pick up rags for?"

"It isn't a rag, Mother Winkyn," said the little boy. "It's your best yellow petticoat."

Mother Winkyn stared at the petticoat in surprise. Yes - it *was* her best Sunday petticoat. But how did it get there? She had left it on the washing line.

"You see," explained the little boy, trotting by her side, "I was playing in the road outside your cottage and I saw the wind blow your petticoat away from the washing line. So I went after it, because I know my mother gets upset when she loses anything. It blew such a long way away – and every time I got close to it the wind blew it away again.

That's how I bumped into you round the corner. The petticoat had just blown round the corner, and I was afraid that if I didn't run very fast I would lose sight of it. I'm really very sorry that I knocked you over. I do hope that I didn't hurt you."

Well! Mother Winkyn really didn't know *what* to say! She did wish she hadn't shouted at the little boy so much. After all, he was only trying to get back some of her blown-away washing for her. He hadn't really meant to knock her over and spill her shopping.

She looked down at the little boy. He was very much out of breath with all his running and his face was very rosy. He really looked a very nice little boy indeed – a very *kind* little boy. It was so nice of him to run after her washing like that – her very best petticoat too. She wouldn't like to lose that.

Suddenly Mother Winkyn felt quite ashamed of herself.

"You're a good little fellow, and I'm very sorry that I shouted at you," she said. "Of course I won't complain to your mother. I'll tell her you're the nicest little boy I know, instead. It was very kind of you to chase after my washing like that. Perhaps one day you would like to come to tea with me. We will have chocolate cake, biscuits and jelly and ice-cream."

Well, what do you think of that? The little boy couldn't believe his ears! But it was all quite true, and the very next day he went to tea with Mother Winkyn and had the loveliest tea he had ever had in his life. His mother went with him and she was very proud when she heard how kind her son had been.

And now Mother Winkyn is quite changed. She smiles at all

the children she meets and gives little treats to the ones she likes best. She has a little tea party for all the children every week and makes chocolate cake and sugar biscuits each time.

The children like her very much and have *quite* forgotten she wasn't always like that! Now they are happy to run errands for her, and they always greet her with a cheerful smile.

Wasn't it a good thing that the little boy was kind enough to run after the washing that blew off the line?

You never know what a kind deed will lead to, do you?

The Smickle-Smockle

ANNA had a birthday, and
her Aunt Jane gave her a
lovely box of coloured plasticine.
Anna was pleased. She showed
the plasticine to her other toys.

"It looks just like coloured
sticks," she said, "but I can make
it into marvellous things. You
just watch me!"

She took a stick of red
plasticine into her hands and
warmed it. Then she began to
squeeze it and work it about
until she had made it into a
round ball. She rolled it across
the playroom floor.

"There!" she said. "I've made
it into a ball! Now watch and see

what I'll make the next stick of plasticine into!"

She took a yellow piece and began to work that about in her hands, too. She squeezed it quite flat, then turned up the sides and smoothed them nicely.

"I'm making a cup to drink from," she told the curly-haired doll. "I've just got to make a little handle for it then it will be finished. Look – don't you think it looks pretty?"

It really was a sweet little cup. It even held water. The toys watched Anna with the greatest interest. A twinkle came into the monkey's eyes. He thought it would be fun to do a little work with the plasticine that night – *he* would make something marvellous! Oh, yes – Monkey always thought he could do wonders!

So that night, when Anna was fast asleep in bed, Monkey took the box of plasticine from the toybox and opened it. He looked at it with his head on one side and thought hard. What should he make? The toys gathered round him to see what he was doing.

"Make a ball, please," said the pink rabbit, looking at the monkey with large glass eyes.

"Then we can all have fun playing with it."

Now the pink rabbit was a timid little thing, and Monkey was fond of teasing him.

"No – I'll make a tiger that will chase you!" he said. The rabbit squealed.

"No, no – I should run away and never come back."

"Then I'll make a red fox with a long bushy tail, and eyes that go like this!" said Monkey, making his eyes big, and glaring at the rabbit.

"Oh, don't look like that," said the rabbit, backing away. "Don't! You're frightening me. Don't make a fox. I really am terribly afraid of them."

"Well – I'll make an owl, a big hooting owl," said Monkey, enjoying himself. "One with great claws that can hold little rabbits, and a voice that goes 'Ooo-ooo-ooo-OOOO!"

"Sh! Sh!" said the big teddy bear. "You'll wake up Anna, you silly, oooohing like that. Be quiet. And don't you dare to make a tiger or a red fox or an owl. You are not to frighten the pink rabbit."

The pink rabbit had run right away to the other end of the playroom when Monkey had hooted like an owl. He had scrambled into the waste-paper basket and hidden himself under some paper. Monkey grinned.

"I won't make a tiger, a red fox or a hooting owl," he said to the teddy. "I'll make something much better."

So, just behind the toy cupboard door, he set to work with the plasticine, and he made a most peculiar animal. It had a small head, a long neck, a perfectly round body with wings, and a long tail like a fish. It had three feet at the front, and what looked like a wheel behind. It really was very strange indeed.

"What is it?" asked the bear. "I've never seen anything at all like that before."

"It's a smickle-smockle," said the monkey, with a grin, adding a pair of cat's ears to the strange-looking creature.

"Well, it's not very pretty," said the teddy, and went off to play ball with the other toys. They played until the daylight began to come in through the nursery window.

"Time to get back into the toy cupboard," said the teddy bear. "Come along, everyone. Monkey, call the pink rabbit. He's still in the paper basket, and if he doesn't come out, he may be emptied into the dustbin."

The monkey watched all the toys getting into the toy cupboard, and then he called to the pink rabbit. "Come out! The sun will soon be up and we must go to sleep."

The pink rabbit poked his big ears out of the basket. He couldn't see a tiger, a red fox or an owl. So he jumped out and ran over the carpet.

"I've got something to show you," said the monkey, and took him behind the cupboard door. There stood the smickle-smockle, looking very fierce because the monkey had cleverly taken two red-headed pins and pressed them into the head for eyes.

"Oooooh! What is it?" said the poor pink rabbit, trembling.

"It's a smickle-smockle!" said the monkey. "Isn't it fierce?"

"What does it eat?" asked the poor pink rabbit, trembling so much that his tail nearly fell off.

"It eats PINK RABBITS!" said the naughty monkey. The rabbit gave a loud squeal and jumped into the toy cupboard in such a hurry that he trod on the clockwork mouse and knocked his key out. He scrambled into the back of the cupboard and sat there, trembling.

"The smickle-smockle will eat me," sobbed the pink rabbit. "He will, he will!"

"The monkey is very naughty to tease you like that," said the bear. "Golly, put the plasticine away and come into the cupboard. AT ONCE!"

The monkey quickly smashed the smickle-smockle together, and squeezed the plasticine into long sticks again. He put them neatly into the box, ready for Anna to play with once more, and then carried the box into the toy cupboard.

"I've put the smickle-smockle

into the box," he said, with a grin. "I hope he won't get out."

"Oh! Oh! Don't put the box in here then, in case he gets out!" wailed the pink rabbit, and he tried to shut himself into the brick box.

"He'll get out if he smells a pink rabbit nearby, but not unless," said the naughty monkey. That made the pink rabbit go nearly mad, and he rushed round and round the toy cupboard, squealing loudly. Everyone got very tired of him.

"You've trodden on my face," said the blue cat.

"And you've stepped twice on

my foot," said the sailor doll. "Settle down there and go to sleep, stupid! Monkey, open the box of plasticine and show the pink rabbit that the smickle-smockle really isn't there, for goodness sake!"

"No, don't open the box, don't open the box!" wailed the trembling rabbit. "The smickle-smockle will jump straight out at me if you do!"

The monkey began to open the lid – and the pink rabbit leapt straight out of the cupboard into the coal-scuttle! And there he had to stay, because by that time it was day, and no toy was allowed to move or speak.

Anna found the pink rabbit in the coal scuttle, and she had to wash him and peg him up on the line in the garden to dry. He was very unhappy because the pegs hurt his ears. He cried when he got back to the toys that night.

"Oh! Oh! Don't put me near the box where the smickle-smockle is!" he wept when the teddy bear welcomed him back. "I can see the box. I shall jump straight into the coal-scuttle again. I shall! I shall!"

"Dear me, this won't do," said the bear, getting quite worried. "Monkey, this is all your silly fault. You must think of some way to make the poor pink rabbit feel better. He has had a dreadful shock."

"Yes, Monkey. You just put things right," said all the toys; and they looked so stern that the monkey quite lost his merry twinkle, and looked scared. It wasn't nice to have every single person against him.

He sat and thought – and then he brightened up. He took the lid off the box of plasticine and beamed at everyone.

"I'm going to make some green lettuces, some red carrots, and some yellow onions," he said.

"Just watch me, and you might see how to do it!"

Everyone watched him. He really was a rather clever monkey. He took the green stick of plasticine and made two fine green lettuces. He made three red carrots, and he made five nice yellow onions. They all looked lovely.

"There you are, Pink Rabbit!" said the monkey. "That's a lot better than a horrible smickle-smockle, isn't it? *There's* a fine feast for you!"

Well, the little pink rabbit really and truly thought that the monkey *had* made him a feast, and before anyone could stop him he ran up to the plasticine vegetables and gobbled up the carrots, the onions and the lettuces! He didn't mind at all that they were plasticine ones. His insides were made of sawdust, so it wasn't likely that the plasticine would upset him.

"Oh!" cried the monkey in horror. "You've eaten Anna's red, yellow and green plasticine! There's only the blue and the orange sticks left. Whatever will she say?"

Well, wasn't that a shock for the toys, especially for Monkey? Most of Anna's plasticine had disappeared into the pink rabbit's tummy!

"You'll have to buy some more," said the bear.

"Where?" asked Monkey, with tears in his eyes. But nobody knew where plasticine could be bought. So they made the monkey empty out his little money-box, and take all his pennies, and put them into the half-empty box of plasticine for Anna to buy some new bits with. Won't she be surprised when she finds them there?

"Monkey won't tease people again in a hurry!" said the teddy bear. "He can't buy ice-creams or chocolates for ages now. His money is all gone!"

It was sad, wasn't it? Poor Monkey didn't smile for at least three nights, he was so upset!

The
Extraordinary
Christmas
Tree

PING came racing into the kitchen, and startled his brother Pong very much.

"Pong! I know where some magic Christmas trees are growing. You know – the kind that flower into all kinds of lovely presents on Christmas Day! Shall we take one tonight?"

"We shouldn't," said Pong. "But all the same – let's do it! I'd love a magic Christmas tree that would grow presents for us on every branch!"

So that night the two bad imps stole through the darkness to where the magic Christmas trees grew in Witch Green-Eyes' garden. They climbed the wall, and slipped down the other side.

Ping had a spade. Pong had a sack. Ping dug up a nice little tree and Pong put it into his sack. Then they climbed back over the wall and ran at top speed to their cottage.

They hid it in the larder, in case anyone saw it. But on Christmas Eve they put it by the fire to warm the magic in it, and make it begin to bud and grow presents for them for the next day. The tree shook its green branches, and the two imps looked hard to see if any buds were growing.

But they couldn't see any. They

went to bed and fell asleep, longing for Christmas Day to come. Santa Claus didn't go near their cottage. He knew quite well that they were bad imps, and he certainly wasn't going to leave them anything in their stockings.

In the middle of the night, Ping woke up. He heard a noise, a kind of windy sound in the kitchen. What could it be?

He got out of bed and went to look. The kitchen was full of the sound of the wind, and the Christmas tree's branches were waving wildly. To Ping's surprise, the tree seemed to be about twice the size it had been!

"Pong!" he called up the stairs. "Come and look at our tree. It has grown tremendously. But there aren't any presents budding on it yet!"

"Oh, go back to bed!" called Pong, sleepily. "If it grows a bit, all the better for us! There will be more room on it for presents!"

So Ping went back to bed and fell asleep again. But early in the morning he was awakened by somebody making a noise on the bedroom floor. At least, that is what it sounded like! He leaned over the edge of the bed to see what it was – and dear me, what a shock he got!

The Christmas tree in the kitchen below was growing through the floor of the bedroom! It had gone right through the kitchen ceiling and was now waving its spiky topmost branch through a hole in the bedroom floor!

"Pong!" cried Ping in alarm. "Quick! Look at the tree! It's grown much too large. We must stop it."

But they couldn't, of course. Instead of taking a magic Christmas tree that grew presents, they had taken one whose magic made it grow enormous, and which could be used for a very big children's party. Witch Green-Eyes sold plenty of those. They didn't grow any presents at all.

Well, Christmas Day was a terrible day for Ping and Pong that year! The tree grew slowly up through the bedroom floor, taking the chest-of-drawers with it and upsetting the wash-stand. It grew right up to the bedroom ceiling.

And then it grew through that, and soon its topmost spike stuck out of the roof beside the chimney-pot. And all the little folk of the village came to stare in surprise.

Ping was crying. "Go and fetch Witch Green-Eyes!" he called to the villagers. "Tell her to get her horrid tree!"

Witch Green-Eyes came to see it. She stood and laughed, and her black cat laughed with her.

"Well, well – it's a fine punishment for two dishonest little thieves!" she said. "I don't want the tree back. You can keep it. I've no doubt it will stop growing soon – when it's taken the roof off your cottage!"

"Please, dear witch, please take it away," begged Pong. "We'll do anything you like if only you'll take it away."

Witch Green-Eyes looked at him sharply. "I'll take it away if you'll come and dig over the ground in my garden, once all the trees have been sold," she said. "It's hard work – but hard work will do you two good."

"We'll come and do the digging. And we'll plant the magic seeds for next year's trees," said Ping.

"Oh, no, you won't," said Witch Green-Eyes. "I'll do that myself. It's easy. You can do all the digging, and that will save me a lot of trouble. Well – I'll take away this tree now."

So she called out a string of magic words and, Hey Presto!

The tree began to shrink back to its original size, a small tree no higher than Ping or Pong. Then the witch fetched it from the kitchen, and she and her cat stalked off, laughing loudly.

As for Ping and Pong, they had to mend their ceilings and roof, because the holes let in the snow and rain, and they didn't like that at all. They were very miserable indeed.

But they cheered up a bit when they got an invitation to a party in the village hall. They put on their best things and went off arm in arm.

But, oh dear, when they got to

the hall, what did they see but the very Christmas tree, again grown enormously high, that they had stolen a few nights before, standing at the end of the hall. And when it saw the bad imps, the tree began to wave its big branches and make such a furious windy noise that the imps were scared and rushed out of the hall at top speed. So they didn't get a present off the tree after all.

And now they have got to go digging in Witch Green-Eyes' garden – but nobody feels a bit sorry for them. Neither do I!

Go Away Bee!

TEDDY was much too fond of sweet things. He knew where the jam was kept, on a low shelf in the kitchen cupboard, and at night, when he thought the toys weren't looking, he would creep downstairs, climb up on the shelf, sit beside the jam pot and dip his paws in.

He always knew if the children had left any sweets about, too, and it did shock the toys to see him helping himself.

"They're not yours," said the big doll. "You know they're not."

"Some of them are now," said Teddy, patting his fat little tummy. "Ooh, they're nice. Have some?"

"Of *course* not," said all the toys at once.

"One of these days you'll be sorry," said the toy soldier.

"I shan't," said Teddy, and took another sweet. "I am never sorry. What's the use?"

"We shan't speak to you!" said the big doll.

"Good," said Teddy. "I always think you toys talk too much. If you don't speak to me or come near me I shall be very glad. You only frown and scold and nag."

"He's hopeless," said the toy soldier, walking off with the others. "A very nasty person."

Now, the next day the children

had bread and honey for tea, and they were very pleased. Teddy stared at the honey pot, at the teaspoon that ladled the yellow honey out, and at the bread and butter so thickly spread with the lovely, sweet, golden stuff.

"Honey! I've never tasted it in my life! I really must try some tonight. If only the children's mother puts the honey on a low shelf in the cupboard!" When she heard him say that the big doll frowned at him. "I know what you're up to, you naughty teddy bear. You're not to touch the honey."

Teddy waited till the toys were

playing hide and seek. Then he
went to hide, too – but he crept
downstairs, of course, and hid in
the cupboard where the honey
had been left next to the jam.
And didn't he have a fine time!

The toys went down and found
him there, fast asleep, when they
had finished playing. He was
leaning up against the honey pot.
They pulled him away.

"Look at his back! All covered
with honey that has dripped
down the jar!" said the big doll,
in disgust. "What *are* we going to
do with him?"

"Leave me alone," said Teddy
sleepily. "You're always stopping

me from having fun. Leave me alone."

"You need a good bath," said the toy soldier. "Your back is all sticky with honey. We'll hold you under the tap."

"No, you won't," said Teddy, in alarm. "If you do I'll go to the brick box and throw every single brick at you. And you know what a good shot I am."

"Oh, leave him," said the big doll, in disgust. "Let him be sticky if he wants to." So they left him, and went back to the playroom. Teddy got up, shook himself awake, and went upstairs to the corner where he usually slept for the night.

It was a fine, sunny day the next day. The children took their toys into the garden. They took the big doll, Teddy, the toy soldier, the pink dog and the black horse. They sat them all down in the grass.

Bees buzzed in the flowers all around. Soon one of them smelt the honey on Teddy's back. It flew up and landed on Teddy's fur.

"Ooh! Ow!" squealed Teddy in fright. "A bee is walking on me! Chase him off, Toy Soldier!"

"Why should I?" asked the toy soldier, with a grin. "He's as fond of honey as you are. He only wants a little off your back, where you're sticky. Let him have it."

"*You* took honey when you wanted it. Why shouldn't the bee?" said the big doll.

"Quite right," said the pink dog.

"Go away, bee!" yelled Teddy, and tried to flick the bee off his back. But he was too fat and couldn't reach right round. The bee stuck fast.

"It might sting me!" wailed Teddy. "Oh, take the bee off somebody!"

But nobody did. They just sat round giggling and enjoying the fun. Ha, ha! Somebody else wanted honey and was getting it.

"Go away, bee!" squealed Teddy, and wriggled his shoulders. "You're tickling me."

The bee flew off, but it came back at once. Teddy got up, turned his back to a fern growing nearby, and rubbed himself against the fronds. The bee flew away.

"Aha! You're off!" cried Teddy. "Now I'm going to lie down flat on the ground - then you can't suck at the honey on my back."

He lay down flat. The bee flew down and tried to crawl underneath. "Mind it doesn't sting you!" called the toy soldier.

The bee managed to creep right under Teddy, and then the poor bear had to sit up because the bee tickled him so.

"GO AWAY, BEE!" he roared. But the bee took absolutely no notice at all.

"He's probably a deaf bee," said the big doll. "How awful, Teddy, you'll have to put up with him till every bit of honey is sucked off your back."

"I'll go to the pond and try to wipe the honey off," groaned Teddy. So, with the bee flying round his head, he made his way to the pond. But he couldn't reach round to his back to splash the water there – and suddenly he lost his balance and fell right into the water!

The big doll ran to rescue him. "Whatever will the children say when they see you?" she said to Teddy. "You're soaked."

"They'll hang you up on the clothes line, pegged by your ears," said the toy soldier. The bear gave a scream.

"Oh no, oh no! Dry me quickly, big doll. Oh, here's that bee again. Go AWAY, bee!"

The bee settled on Teddy's nose. The bear smacked at it with his wet paw. The bee at

once stung Teddy on the nose,
and he fell into the pond again,
yelling loudly. The bee flew
away, scared.

"Poor Teddy," said the big doll,
and pulled him out of the water
again. "I'd say he's been punished
enough. We must dry him before
the children come back."

So they dried him. Then he sat
down in the sun to get warm.
There was no honey on his back
now, because it had all been
wiped off in the drying.

"I'll never steal again," said
Teddy solemnly. Then he
suddenly looked scared.
"What's this great big thing in

front of my eyes?" he asked.

"It's your nose," said the toy soldier, and giggled. "The bee stung it and it's all swollen up. You do look funny!"

He did, poor bear. The children couldn't *imagine* what was the matter with him, and nobody liked to tell them.

The Silly Monkey

THERE was once a handsome toy monkey who was very proud of himself. He wore a red coat and blue trousers, and round his neck was a very fine yellow scarf that tied in a big bow in front. He was very vain about this scarf, and was always asking the other toys if it looked really nice.

"Oh, do be quiet," the teddy bear would say crossly. "That's the third time you've asked me the same silly question today! You don't deserve such a nice scarf if you're so vain about it! One of these days you'll lose it and that will serve you right."

"Lose it!" said Monkey, scornfully. "You don't know what you're talking about, Teddy! Why, it's tied in a tight bow round my neck, and there's a pin in the front to keep it straight. Don't you think it's a perfectly beautiful scarf, and that it suits me very well indeed?"

"There you go again!" said Teddy impatiently. "That's the fourth time you've asked me. Now, do be quiet."

Monkey left him and went to look at himself in the mirror that was in the doll's house. He patted his red coat, smoothed down his blue trousers and then

admired his beautiful yellow tie
for the hundredth time. He
thought he must be the best-
looking and best-dressed
monkey in the whole world!

Now that night the toys held a
tea-party in the doll's house. The
curly-haired doll laid the table
and set out the little white and
blue cups. Then Teddy brought
some tiny jam sandwiches and
little chocolate cakes. The
clockwork clown made the tea,
and everything was ready.

At the last minute the clown
found that there were not
enough cups. Someone would
have to go without. As all the

toys were feeling annoyed with Monkey and his vain ways, they said *he* could go without his tea.

"It's just as well!" said Teddy with a grin. "You might spill some tea down that beautiful scarf of yours, you know, Monkey!"

"I'm *going* to have some tea to drink," said the monkey crossly, hating to be left out.

"Well, there's no cup for you," said the curly-haired doll, busy handing round the cakes and sandwiches.

"Then I shall find a cup for myself," said Monkey angrily and he rushed off. What do you think he had thought of? It was the silver thimble out of Lucy's little work basket! Lucy was the little girl they belonged to and Monkey thought her thimble would make a splendid cup, far better than the little china ones that the other toys were drinking from.

But when Teddy saw what Monkey was doing, he called out to him at once.

"Monkey! You mustn't take things out of Lucy's basket! She would be very cross with you! You can't have her little silver thimble!"

"Oh, *can't* I!" said the silly Monkey, and he made a rude

face at the bear. "Well, I can, so there! Here it is, see! And I'm going to pour myself out a cup of tea and drink it from this dear little thimble!"

He took hold of the teapot and poured some tea into the thimble. The toys watched him in dismay. It really was very naughty of Monkey, for none of them were allowed to meddle with Lucy's things. All the toys were very fond of her.

Now, just as Monkey was walking to his seat, feeling very pleased with himself, his head held high, he caught his foot in a corner of the rug. Over he went, smack! The little thimble of tea was spilt on the floor, and the thimble itself rolled right away!

"Ooh! Ow! I've hurt myself!" wept Monkey, rubbing his knee.

"It serves you right," said the curly-haired doll. "You should look where you are going. If you *will* walk with your head in the air, you must expect to fall over."

"Where's the thimble?" asked Monkey getting up. He looked around for it but he couldn't see it. "Did anyone see where it went?" he asked anxiously. But nobody had.

"I *think* it rolled into that corner over there," said the

teddy bear, pointing. So the monkey ran to look. But all he found was a hole in the floorboards! And oh, dear me, shining beneath the boards was the little thimble! It had rolled down the hole and there it was.

Monkey tried to get it, but he couldn't. It was too far down. Whatever could he do?

"I can't reach it," he said, half crying. "Teddy, come and see if you can get it."

But none of the toys could reach it. They stood round the hole and looked down at the little thimble, wondering what on Earth they could do.

"Lucy will be very upset when she finds her nice little silver thimble is gone," said the curly-haired doll. "It was very naughty of you to take it, Monkey."

"I *must* get it back, I *must*!" cried Monkey. "Oh, whatever shall I do?"

"Let's call the little brown mouse who lives behind the wall over there," said the clockwork clown. "Perhaps he will be able to get it for us."

So they called him and he came, his bright black eyes shining, and his little nose moving up and down. They showed him where the thimble was, down the hole.

"Can you get it?" Monkey asked.

"Easily," said the brown mouse. "There's a little tunnel that leads from my own hole to this one, and I can get the thimble in my mouth, carry it to my hole and then bring it out to you."

"Oh, *please* go and get it!" cried Monkey at once, delighted.

"But what will you give me, if I do?" asked the mouse.

"Anything, anything!" said the monkey, looking round. "The doll's pretty brooch – the key belonging to the clockwork clown – the bonnet off the baby doll."

"I don't want any of those,"
said the brown mouse, looking at
the monkey. "I want something
belonging to you."

"What's that?" asked Monkey.

"I'd like that yellow scarf of
yours," said the little mouse. "I
could use it to make a lovely nest
for my family. It would help keep
us warm all winter. Will you give
it to me?"

"Certainly *not*!" cried Monkey,
suddenly in a rage. "Why, it's the
most beautiful scarf in the whole
world."

"Just right to build a nest
with," said the mouse. "Well, if
you won't give it to me, I shan't

get the thimble for you, so goodbye!"

He ran to his hole – but the other toys surrounded Monkey and spoke angrily to him.

"You were quite ready to give away the doll's pretty brooch, and the clown's key!" they cried. "But as soon as something of *yours* is asked for, you say no! You are a horrid, selfish, vain monkey, and you *shall* give the mouse your yellow scarf!"

The clown suddenly snatched at the yellow scarf and undid it. He dragged it off Monkey's neck and ran to the mouse's hole.

"Little brown mouse!" he

called. "Here is the scarf you wanted. Please come and get the thimble for us."

At once the mouse appeared, and took the scarf. He wrapped it round his neck several times and tied a most beautiful bow under his whiskery chin. He looked too sweet for words, and all the toys smiled to see him. Then he ran down his hole again, found the thimble and brought it safely back. He gave it to the clown, danced round in delight a few times, showing off his fine yellow bow, and then disappeared down the hole to show his family what a fine warm nest they would have for the winter.

The clown put the thimble back into the work basket. He looked at Monkey who was crying in a corner, feeling dreadful without his yellow bow.

"Nobody will like me without my yellow scarf," he groaned.

"Well, nobody liked you *with* it!" said Teddy. "Cheer up! You won't be vain any more and we will like you lots better."

It was perfectly true – they really did!

The Land of
P s and Q s

ONCE upon a time there lived a little boy called Donald, who would never say "thank you." Sometimes he remembered "please," but only when he wanted something very badly, and thought he wouldn't get it unless he said "please." So you can see he wasn't a very polite little boy. This is the story of how he was cured.

Now one day Donald was playing by himself in a field at the back of his house. It was about eleven o'clock in the morning, and it suddenly seemed to Donald that he had had his breakfast a very long time ago.

"I'm so hungry!" he said. "Perhaps I'd better go home and see if it's dinner time."

"No, don't do that!" said a voice over the hedge. "Come and join us in our picnic, won't you?"

Donald looked over the hedge in surprise. He saw four little men, dressed in red. They were sitting on the ground, eating enormous currant buns that had a delicious, freshly-baked smell.

"Oh!" said Donald, sniffing. "Your buns *do* smell good! I'd love to join you!"

Donald climbed over the hedge, and sat down beside the little red men.

In the middle was a large dish of buns. The biggest man handed it politely to Donald. He took the very biggest one on the dish, and began eating it, without saying a single "thank you."

The little man stared at Donald strangely, and put the plate down. Then he went on eating his own bun.

Soon Donald had finished. He was still hungry. "I want another bun," he said, and reached out to the dish. He didn't even *think* of saying "please."

The red men stared at one another and said nothing. One of them handed the dish to Donald, who took a bun and again forgot to say "thank you."

"What a disgusting little boy!" said Rab, the chief little red man, when Donald had eaten all his cake. "He can't even say 'thank you!' We must certainly try to cure him!"

"Let's take him to the land of P's and Q's!" said another little man. "He'll soon be cured then!"

Donald jumped up. "I *won't* go to that horrid country!" he cried. "I'm going home, so there!"

"All right. Just you try and go home!" said Rab.

Donald turned and tried to walk to the hedge.

"Oh!" he cried, "my feet won't move! It's magic! Let me go!"

"No, you must come with us," said Rab, getting up. "We cure ever so many boys and girls who won't say 'please' or 'thank you.' You'll be much nicer when you come back."

Donald felt frightened. He was much too big to cry, of course, but he felt very like crying when the little red men surrounded him, put their hands on his shoulders, and marched him off through the woods.

They went right into the heart of the woods, until they reached a ring of very large toadstools.

"Sit down on one, Donald," said Rab, "and hold tight."

All the little men chose a toadstool, and sat down near Donald. Donald had a big toadstool, and held tight as Rab had told him.

"One, two, three,
And down go we!"
shouted Rab suddenly. Donald felt his toadstool sinking quickly into the ground, and he saw that all the others were too.

Down and down he went, seeing nothing at all, for it was quite dark. Then bump! His toadstool came to a stop in a great cave, lit by swinging blue lamps.

All the others were there too, and they jumped off their toadstools just as Donald did.

"Come on, Donald!" they cried. "This way!"

They led him through the blue cave, until they came to another cave, this time lit by green lamps. A pair of very small railway lines ran through it.

"Oh, a railway! Where does it go to?" asked Donald, astonished.

"All sorts of places!" answered Rab. "You can get to any part of Fairyland by the Gnome Railway."

Suddenly a little engine came out of the darkness, pulling odd-looking carriages behind it. They had no roofs and no seats - just cushions on the floor for passengers to sit on.

"Jump in!" cried Rab, pushing Donald into a carriage as the train stopped. All the little men got in and chose cushions. Off went the train again.

After a long time, and after they had passed a lot of stations with strange-sounding names, the train left the caves and came out into the open air. Fiddlestick Field, Breezy Corner and Pool-in-the-Hollow were some of the stations that they went through, and Donald longed to get out

and explore, for he knew he was
in Fairyland. At some of the
stations there were fairies and
elves, pixies and gnomes, and
they looked very exciting with
their shining wings.

At last the train slowed down
again."P's and Q's! P's and Q's!"
shouted a Gnome porter.

"Jump out quickly, Donald!"
said Rab. The little men jumped
out, and Donald with them.

He found himself in a field of
beautiful flowers, and just by him
was a big sign-post:
TO THE LAND OF P's AND Q's

"Follow the path over the
field," said Rab, "and go straight

ahead. Go to the Yellow Castle and ask for Giant Politesse. He'll tell you what to do. You can go home again if you can find the Courteous Gate and go through it safely! I'll be waiting for you on the other side, and I'll take you home again."

The little men jumped into the waiting train, waved their hands, and off they went, leaving poor Donald alone.

Donald stared after them, feeling very lonely. When the train had disappeared from view, he went over the field, and came at last to a stile. In the distance he saw a big yellow castle on a hill.

"Oh, that must be the castle where Giant Politesse lives!" thought Donald. "I hope he'll be kind to me, and let me go home!"

When he arrived at the castle, he found the giant sitting outside the front door. He was a huge giant, with kind blue eyes and the most wonderful manners. Donald didn't feel at all afraid of him, and told him all about Rab, and how the little red men had brought him to Fairyland.

"Oh, do let me go home!" he begged at the end.

"No, you can't go home till you've learned to be polite!" said Giant Politesse. "You must stay here awhile. Go to the kitchen, and ask my servants if they will have you as kitchen boy. They will teach you to be polite, and then you can go home."

Donald went sadly to the kitchen, where there was a great clattering of pots and pans. There were the strangest little beings there. Some of them were dressed in blue overalls and caps which had a big "P" embroidered on them. Some of them had purple overalls, and these had "Q" embroidered on them.

"I suppose these are the P's and Q's," thought Donald, standing and watching them.

Then he said out loud, "Can I be your kitchen boy, and help you?"

"Did Giant Politesse send you?" asked one.

"Yes," he said, "so do let me."

"Well, sit down," said the cook, "we're just going to have dinner."

Donald sat down at a long table and watched the cook ladling out meat and potatoes.

"Will you have a potato, Donald?" asked the cook.

"Yes, a big one," he answered, forgetting to say "please."

And then what *do* you think happened? The largest potato in the dish jumped straight out, flew to Donald, and hit him on the chest! And there it stayed!

"Oh, oh! Help!" yelled Donald,
trying to get the potato off.

"You forgot to say please," said
the cook. "That sort of thing
always happens in the Land of
P's and Q's to anyone who
forgets to be polite! You won't be
able to get it off till you pass
through the Courteous Gate on
your way home."
It was quite true. That potato
wouldn't come off, so Donald
had to let it stay there. He was
very upset about it.

"Here is your meat!" said the
cook, handing a plate to Donald.
He took it and set it down in

front of him – and will you believe it – he didn't say "thank you!"

Up jumped the meat, splashing the gravy all over Donald, and landing on his sleeve! There it stayed, and Donald couldn't get it off.

"Well, you *are* a little stupid!" cried the P's and Q's. "You forgot to say 'thank you!'"

Poor Donald nearly cried with frustration, he was so hungry and wanted his dinner. He was very careful to say "please" and "thank you" for his pudding and he ate it up hungrily.

After dinner, Donald helped to

wash up all the plates. One dish was very sticky and horrid, and he *could* not get it clean.

"Give it to me; I'll do it for you," said a P kindly. Donald handed him the dish without a word. Clap! The plate jumped straight out of the P's hand, and landed on Donald's head!

"Oh! You didn't thank me for saying I'd help you!" exclaimed the P. "Now look what the plate's done!"

Well, Donald couldn't get that plate off, so you can imagine how strange he looked with a potato and some meat on his chest and sleeve, and a plate on his head.

"Oh dear, oh dear! I must be careful," cried Donald. "I'd no idea I forgot so often!"

He tried very hard to remember after that. The P's and Q's were very kind to him, and when he didn't know how to do anything, they would always show him. Donald thought they were very nice, and he began to think it would be rather jolly if he could be nice like that too!

It is hard to be nice with a cold potato sticking on your chest, and a stupid plate balanced on your head, but Donald managed it. He only forgot once, and that was when a Q came running in with a little grey kitten in his arms.

"Look!" he cried. "Here's a darling little baby kitten."

All the P's and Q's rushed to see. Donald rushed too, but he was last and could see nothing.

He pushed his way through to the front. "Let *me* see! Let *me* see!" he cried.

"Don't push! It's rude!" said the cook. Then, swish! The kitten jumped up on to Donald's shoulder, and stayed there.

"Now look what's happened!" cried a Q. "You were rude, and the little kitten will stay on your shoulder till you're polite! Poor little kitten!"

So Donald had to carry the little, mewing, scratching kitten on his shoulder all evening. He was very upset, because he felt that it was very unkind to the kitten as well as being uncomfortable for himself.

Donald lived in the castle for two or three days, trying hard to be as polite and kind as the P's and Q's. He tried to help them and to do all he could to make himself a really nice little boy.

He forgot to say "please" only once when he wanted some chocolate, and that jumped down his neck, and felt very uncomfortable – and another

time he took too much treacle
with his pudding, and you can
guess what he felt like when *that*
jumped at him! He was sticky all
day after that, for he couldn't get
rid of it.

One morning Donald felt very
tired, for the day before he had
cleaned six pairs of Giant
Politesse's boots, and as they
were each quite as big as an
ordinary bath, he had worked
hard. He decided he would have
a good rest the next morning,
and do something easy.

"I'll clean the spoons!" he
thought. So he sat down and
began. But presently in came the

cook, holding his head and
moaning.

"Oh, oh! My head does ache!
And I've got to go out in the hot
sun, and tell the butcher to send
the meat at twelve o'clock,"
moaned the cook.

"I'll go for you," said Donald,
jumping up.

"But you're tired, and it's a
long way!" said the cook.

"Never mind. I'll go for you!"
said Donald. "Go and lie down,
and perhaps you'll feel better."

"Well, it's very kind of you, and
thank you very much!" said the
cook. "Go down the road for a
mile, then up the Crooked Hill.

The butcher lives at the top. Please give him my message, and tell him I couldn't come myself."

Off went Donald in the hot sun, down the road for a mile, and then over the fields to Crooked Hill. By the time he got there he was so tired he could hardly walk! He gave his message to the butcher, who seemed very much surprised to see a boy with a kitten, a potato, a plate and meat all hanging about him.

"And *please* could you tell me a short way back?" asked Donald.

"Go down the hill, and over the stile," said the butcher. "That will be much shorter."

Down went Donald, and over the stile. And what do you think he saw on the other side of the stile? Why, a great gate, and over it were these words:

The Courteous Gate

It was shut. Donald peered through it and saw a blue plane in a field beyond the gate. Then he saw Rab, the little red man, peeping through the gate at him.

"Are you cured yet?" asked Rab. "My! You do look funny! What a pity you've got a plate on your head, it looks so strange!"

"*Please* open the gate, and let me through," begged Donald.

"Knock three times on it," said Rab. "If you're cured it will open for you."

Donald knocked three times, and waited, trembling, hoping the gate would open.

Creak! Creak! Creak! Slowly the gate opened little by little, until there was room for Donald to pass through! As he walked through, whizz-z-z! Off flew the plate, down dropped the potato and meat, and away ran the kitten! The last remains of the chocolate down his neck and the sticky treacle disappeared, and there was Donald, quite free from all the things that he had carried about for days!

"Hurray!" shouted Donald, jumping about with joy. "Do take me home, please, Rab, will you? I'm quite cured now, truly!"

"You wouldn't have found the Courteous Gate if you hadn't done someone a good turn," chuckled Rab. "So I know you must be cured. Come on! Jump into the plane, and I'll land you in your back garden in no time!"

Off they went up in the air, and down again slowly, and, bump! the plane came to rest.

"It's my own garden! Oh, thank you, Rab!" cried Donald. "Now I *must* go and tell Mummy all about it!"

He rushed off to find his Mummy, and oh, how glad she was to see him. She could hardly believe he had really been to the Land of P's and Q's, but when she found that he was always polite and kind, and NEVER forgot a "please" or a "thank you," she knew what he said was true.

But I'm rather glad that when *I* sometimes forget to say thank you for a cake, it doesn't jump off the plate at me, aren't you?